ELI'S MAGIC MOMENT

By Kevin Poplawski

Illustrated by Michael Rausch

LIAM,

MAKE THAT

MAGIC MOMENT!

(handwritten signature)

To Elizabeth, Emily and Hailey...
my love and my inspiration.
— K.P.

To Kim... hello!
— M.R.

Eli was an elephant,
the **biggest** one of all.
He loved many kinds of sports,
but most especially basketball.

Eli was on the Trekkers' team,
but he didn't get to play.
Every one of his teammates
was better in EVERY way.

Barry Buck could pass the ball,
and help the team play better.

Cooper Cow played great defense,
and he was a real go-getter.

Frankie Fox was a shooter,
he could score from anywhere.

Lewis Lion grabbed rebounds,
then hid the ball in his hair!

Poor Eli was just so very slow.
He couldn't dribble, shoot, or dunk.

So all the fans and players
thought he really, really stunk.

Ollie Ostrich was their coach,
and a very good coach was he.

Ollie often encouraged Eli
to be all that he could be.

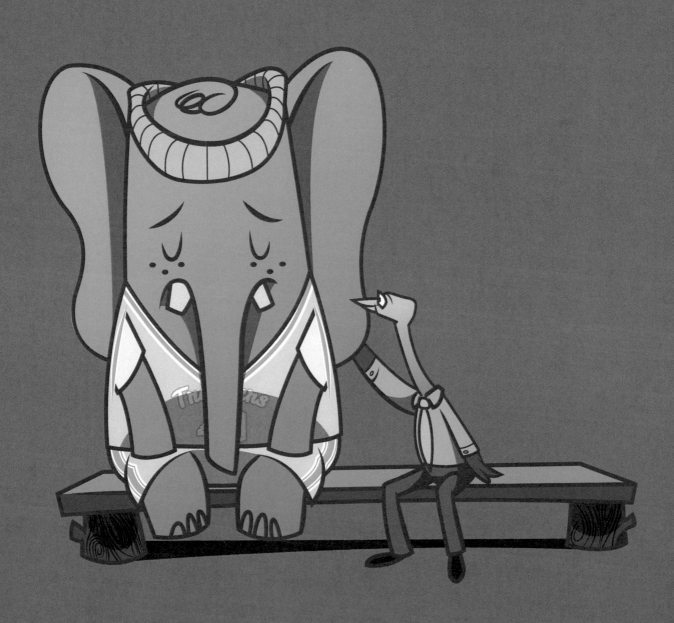

But Eli was just so clumsy
and made many a mistake.
He once sat on a player
and squashed him like a pancake.

The Junglers took on the Trekkers
at this year's Safari Game.

The Junglers had Larry Leopard
and he was in the Hall of Fame.

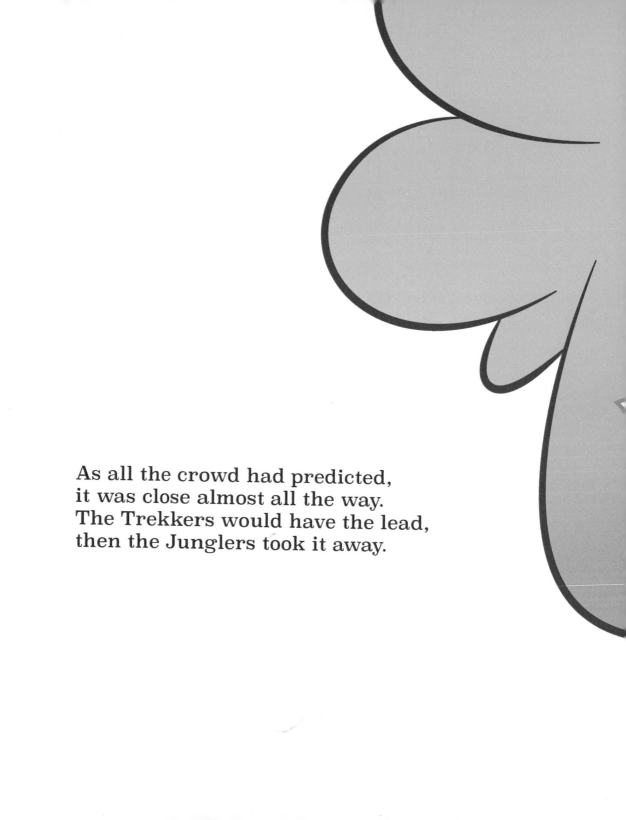

As all the crowd had predicted,
it was close almost all the way.
The Trekkers would have the lead,
then the Junglers took it away.

Lewis Lion hurt his ankle.
It was very late in the game.

So Ollie needed a substitute
and he called out Eli's name!

The players all look confused
The fans all scratched their chin
"This game is much too close Coach,
You can't put Eli in!"

But Coach Ollie had a plan,
that no one knew but him.
Eli was his secret weapon
who was going to help them win!

Larry Leopard took the winning shot,
as he jumped up for a dunk.

But Eli knew what he had to do and blocked it with his trunk.

Eli grabbed the ball
and the Trekkers won the game!
Everyone cheered for Eli
and began to chant his name.

Ollie was so proud of Eli,
he hugged his star with pride,
"I knew you could do it, Eli,
I was always on your side!"

Eli looked his coach in the eyes
and he smiled for all to see,
"I just wanted to thank you, Coach,
because you believed in me."

Made in the USA
Columbia, SC
09 January 2019